Rock, Brock, and the Savings Shock

Sheila Bair

Illustrated by **Barry Gott**

Albert Whitman & Company, Morton Grove, Illinois

To Preston and Colleen—S.B.

To Finn and Nandi—B.G.

This is the tale of Rock and Brock,
twins as different as ball and block.

Rock ate good food. Brock gobbled junk.
Rock liked to bathe. Brock kind of stunk.
Rock studied hard. Brock watched TV.
Rock rose at dawn—Brock slept till three.

Rock was a nearly perfect guy,
but here's the thing: he loved to buy.
His brother, Brock, lived like a slob,
but saved his money by the gob.

One day their gramps, a kindly man,
proposed to them a savings plan.
"For ten straight weeks each Saturday,
I'll give you each one dollar's pay
to mow my lawn and wash my car.
These simple chores will get you far
because I'll do a little trick:
each buck you save, I'll match it quick!
Spend it—there's no extra dough,
so save your cash and watch it grow!"

Then Gramps paid out, true to his word,
one buck to each. Here's what occurred:

A PENNY
SAVED
IS A
PENNY
EARNED

The next week, Gramps gave out more bread—
one dollar each, just as he said.
Rock had one; Brock now had two.
Brock saved his dough; Rock wanted to . . .

but couldn't resist the urge to buy
a giant wind-up tsetse fly.

The third week, Gramps paid out some more.
He matched Brock's two bills up to four.
Rock got one 'cause he had no savings;
still he gave in to spending cravings!

After all, what can a guy do,
with half-price off on green hair goo?

On week four, Brock's dough redoubled:
four to eight — Rock was befuddled.

Rock got one buck, which he promptly spent
on wax fangs tasting like peppermint.

The next week Brock was tempted to buy
an awesome toy he wanted to try—
a rocket ship with a pop-off hatch.
But if he bought it, he'd lose his match.

He stopped himself when he reached the store,
and so Gramps paid him eight bucks more.

With nada for savings, Rock got just one.
He bought some broccoli-flavored gum.

Gramps paid out from summer to fall.
While Brock saved his, Rock spent it all.
He found toys for a dime at a yard sale—
a car with three wheels, a polka-dot snail.

He bought such bargains with his cash—
clown ears, fruit hat, a big moustache!
Soon Rock, the neater of the boys,
found himself waist-deep in toys.

Super
Marmoset

But Brock's cash grew and grew and grew—
eight, then sixteen, then thirty-two.
His pile of bucks became so great,
he had to store them in a crate!

Ten weeks went by. Poor Rock was doomed.
He had no cash; Brock's had ballooned!
With matching dollars, at the end,
Brock had five hundred twelve to spend!

Brock used his cash to buy nice things:
a telescope to see Saturn's rings,
a book for Mom, a shirt for Dad,
for Gramps a robe of tartan plaid.

With fifty bucks left, what did Brock do?
He opened a bank account for two—
a joint account for him and his bro,
a place to keep their hard-earned dough.

'Cause Brock ate junk and hated his bath,
but one thing he knew, he knew his math.
He saved his money like a miser,
and of the twins, he proved the wiser.

By seeing Brock's humongous take,
Rock finally realized his mistake.
From that day on, he saved his loot
and gave up on his spending toot.

The twins stashed bucks in their account;
for years and years they watched them mount.
By the time both had gray hair,
they found that they were millionaires!

Do the Math

Seeing is believing. Take a look at how Gramps's savings plan turned $1 into $512 in just ten weeks.

	Brock Saved	Gramps Matched	Brock's Total
Week One		$1	$1
Week Two	$1	$1	$2
Week Three	$2	$2	$4
Week Four	$4	$4	$8
Week Five	$8	$8	$16
Week Six	$16	$16	$32
Week Seven	$32	$32	$64
Week Eight	$64	$64	$128
Week Nine	$128	$128	$256
Week Ten	$256	$256	$512

Now what would happen if, before Saturday of week five, Brock had bought that awesome rocket? Let's say the rocket costs $7, leaving Brock with only $1 in savings.

	Brock Saved	Gramps Matched	Brock's Total
Week One		$1	$1
Week Two	$1	$1	$2
Week Three	$2	$2	$4
Week Four	$4	$4	$8
Brock buys the rocket for $7, leaving $1 in savings.			
Week Five	$1	$1	$2
Week Six	$2	$2	$4
Week Seven	$4	$4	$8
Week Eight	$8	$8	$16
Week Nine	$16	$16	$32
Week Ten	$32	$32	$64

Because Brock reduces his savings, he reduces the amount Gramps matches on week five and all the following weeks. The result is that Brock's total is $64—$448 less than the $512 he would have received by saving it all. That's a big difference!

So You Want to Be a Millionaire?

Unfortunately, most of us don't have wealthy grandpas who will match our savings each week. But banks will keep your money safe and give you a little extra money every year. The extra is called **interest.**

Interest is a percentage of the amount you save for one year. Let's say that when you were born, your parents put $2,000 in a bank account for you at 5 percent interest. That means that after a year, the bank would pay the account $100 in interest, because 5 percent of $2,000 equals 100.

$$5\% \times \$2,000 = \$100$$

So then you would have a total of $2,100 — the $2,000 you started with plus the $100 interest.

$$\$2,000 + \$100 = \$2,100$$

Now let's say all that money is left in the bank for another year. At the end of the second year, the bank would pay another 5 percent interest, except this time, it would be paying interest on $2,100, not $2,000. So it would pay 5 percent of $2,100 or $105.

$$5\% \times \$2,100 = \$105$$

Add that to the $2,100 already there for a total of $2,205.

$$\$2,100 + \$105 = \$2,205$$

If your parents left that money in the bank for you for many years, it would grow into a really big amount. This is because, year after year, the bank would be paying interest on the first $2,000 plus all that had been earned in the past interest payments.

Brock's money grew into such a shocking sum because each week his gramps was matching a bigger amount of money. First he matched $1; the next week, $2; the next week, $4; the next week, $8; and so on. It works the same way at the bank. First it pays interest on $2,000, then $2,100, then $2,205, and so on. The amount gets bigger because the bank is paying you interest on your interest. This is called **compound interest.**

What would happen if after you finished school, you just decided to leave that money in the bank to let it grow? By the time you had gray hair at age sixty-five, the original $2,000 would have grown into nearly $50,000. Now suppose that you not only left that first $2,000 in the bank for sixty-five years, but that each year you added another $2,000. After sixty-five years, you would have over one million dollars!

You don't have to be a financial wizard (or go on a TV show) to become a millionaire. As Rock finally learned, you just have to stop spending all your money and save.

Sheila's Six Saving Tricks

Gramps's summer savings plan turned both Rock and Brock into lifetime savers. Here are some tricks to help you become a lifetime saver, too.

TAKE OUT TEN: Save at least 10 percent of your allowance every week. Ten percent is easy to figure—just cross out a zero. For instance, if your weekly allowance is $5.00, you would save $.50. If it is $6.00, you save $.60.

SPEED SAVE: Ask your parents to give you 10 percent of your allowance separately. For example, if your weekly allowance is $5.00, make sure they give you some of it in quarters so you can put $.50. or two quarters, in your piggy bank right away. Once the money is safe in your bank, you will be less likely to spend it.

GET A SAVINGS BONUS: Ask your parents if they will give you a little extra money every time you save. Every week you save your 10 percent, they could give you an extra quarter. (Of course, you will have to agree to leave that money in your bank and not spend it later.)

SEE-THROUGH SAVINGS: Use a clear container for your savings. It's fun to watch your pile of cash grow as you put more money in each week. The more you save, the more you will want to save.

BE A FUSSBUDGET: Plan each week how you will spend your allowance while saving at least 10 percent. Then stick to the plan! If you think ahead about how you will spend your money, it will be easier to save and you will buy things you really want, instead of silly things (like giant wind-up trotan flies . . .).

COMPOUND YOUR INTEREST: Open a savings account so the bank can start paying you compound interest. Many banks have special accounts for kids that you can open with just a few dollars, and these accounts pay a little bit of interest, too.

Interest rates go up and down. Right now, the interest banks pay on savings accounts is low, so don't be disappointed. After you have saved $25, you can take that money out of your bank account and buy a U.S. government savings bond, which will pay you a higher rate of interest. Ask your bank about government savings bonds or go to this web site: http://www.publicdebt.treas.gov/sav/savkids.htm. Learn about "I" bonds or "EE" bonds. Both are good places for money kids plan to save for many years.

Sheila Bair has spent most of her career in jobs relating to money, working at places like the New York Stock Exchange, the U.S. Treasury Department, and the Federal Deposit Insurance Corporation, where she is now chairman. Though she knows a lot about money, it took her a long time to figure out that it can be as much fun to save as to spend. She and her family love to save things like seashells, bottle caps, pretty rocks, old stamps, and, of course, 10 percent of the money they make through their allowances and jobs. Sheila wants all kids to be savers and hopes that every one of you will be a millionaire by the time you are sixty-five.

Barry Gott has illustrated several children's books, including *Santa's Secrets Revealed* by James Solheim, and *What Do Teachers Do?* by Anne Bowen. His web site is www.barrygott.com. He lives in Cleveland, Ohio, with his wife, kids, cats, and gecko.

Library of Congress Cataloging-in-Publication Data

Bair, Sheila.
Rock, Brock, and the savings shock / by Sheila Bair ; illustrated by Barry Gott.
p. cm.
Summary: Gramps teaches his twin grandsons the value of saving money when he pays each a dollar a week to help with summer chores, then matches every dollar each boy saves.
ISBN-13: 978-0-8075-7094-4 (hardcover)
ISBN-10: 0-8075-7094-X (hardcover)
[1. Saving and investment—Fiction. 2. Twins—Fiction. 3. Brothers—Fiction. 4. Grandfathers—Fiction.
5. Stories in rhyme.] I. Gott, Barry, ill. II. Title.
PZ8.3.B1568Roc 2006 [E]—dc22 2005026974

The text type is set in Tekton.
The design is by Barry Gott and Carol Gildar.

For more information about Albert Whitman & Company, visit our web site at www.albertwhitman.com.